WE BOTH READ®

Parent's Introduction

Whether your child is a beginning reader, a reluctant reader, or an eager reader, this book offers a fun and easy way to encourage and help your child in reading.

Developed with reading education specialists, *We Both Read* books invite you and your child to take turns reading aloud. You read the left-hand pages of the book, and your child reads the right-hand pages—which have been written at one of six early reading levels. The result is a wonderful new reading experience and faster reading development!

You may find it helpful to read the entire book aloud yourself the first time, then invite your child to participate the second time. As you read, try to make the story come alive by reading with expression. This will help to model good fluency. It will also be helpful to stop at various points to discuss what you are reading. This will help increase your child's understanding of what is being read.

In some books, a few challenging words are introduced in the parent's text, distinguished with **bold** lettering. Pointing out and discussing these words can help to build your child's reading vocabulary. If your child is a beginning reader, it may be helpful to run a finger under the text as each of you reads. Please also notice that a "talking parent" ☺ icon precedes the parent's text, and a "talking child" ☺ icon precedes the child's text.

If your child struggles with a word, you can encourage "sounding it out," but keep in mind that not all words can be sounded out. Your child might pick up clues about a word from the picture, other words in the sentence, or any rhyming patterns. If your child struggles with a word for more than five seconds, it is usually best to simply say the word.

Most of all, remember to praise your child's efforts and keep the reading fun. After you have finished the book, ask a few questions and discuss what you have read together. Rereading this book multiple times may also be helpful for your child.

Try to keep the tips above in mind as you read together, but don't worry about doing everything right. Simply sharing the enjoyment of reading together will increase your child's reading skills and help to start your child off on a lifetime of reading enjoyment!

Museum Day

A We Both Read Book

Level K

We Both Read® is a trademark of Treasure Bay, Inc.

Published by
Treasure Bay, Inc.
P.O. Box 119
Novato, CA 94948 USA

Printed in Singapore

Library of Congress Control Number: 2012938789

Hardcover ISBN: 978-1-60115-265-7
Paperback ISBN: 978-1-60115-266-4

We Both Read® Books
Patent No. 5,957,693

Visit us online at:
www.webothread.com

PR-11-13

WE BOTH READ®

Museum Day

By Sindy McKay

Illustrated by Meredith Johnson

TREASURE BAY

Museum Day is here! We ride there on a . . .

. . . bus.

My dad and I can't wait! This day is just for . . .

 . . . us.

Velociraptor

The dinosaurs are great. And some are really . . .

. . . big.

We see some bones and fossils. They even let us . . .

8

. . . dig.

There is a big blue whale. There is a small red . . .

. . . fox.

And meteors from space! To me they look like . . .

. . . rocks.

At noon we stop for lunch. Beneath a tree we . . .

. . . sit.

A birdie steals my sandwich. And then she
shares a . . .

16

. . . bit!

But I don't really mind. I want to go back . . .

. . . in.

I run to see the masks. They always make me . . .

. . . grin.

We look at telephones. We look at lots of . . .

. . . hats.

Egyptian stuff is cool! Egyptians loved their . . .

. . . cats.

We hear a noise — oh, look! A bird is on the . . .

. . . duck.

That birdie stole my lunch. Oh dear, I think he's . . .

. . . stuck!

A guard now has a net. Another hollers, . . .

. . . "NO!"

The bird flies way up high. They need that
bird to . . .

. . . go!

I wave a piece of bread. His wings begin to . . .

. . . flap.

He follows me outside. The guests all cheer and . . .

. . . clap!

And now it's time to go. We see the setting . . .

. . . sun.

But we'll come back again. We always have such . . .

. . . fun!

If you liked **Museum Day,** here are some other
We Both Read® books you are sure to enjoy!

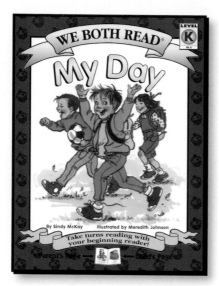

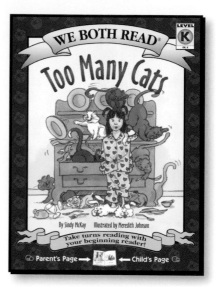

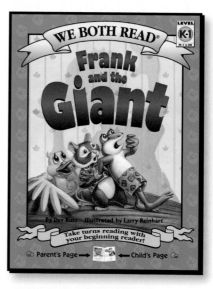